MURDER, FISH, AND NORWAY

MURDER, FISH, AND NORWAY

Glenn EJ Williams

Library of Congress Control Number:		2022918783
ISBN:	Hardcover	978-1-6698-5101-1
	Softcover	978-1-6698-5100-4
	eBook	978-1-6698-5099-1

Print information available on the last page.

Rev. date: 10/11/2022

To order additional copies of this book, contact:
Xlibris
844-714-8691
www.Xlibris.com
Orders@Xlibris.com
847688

For Mom and Dad
I miss you every day.

Hindsight is used by those with awareness.
Foresight is used by those with wisdom.
Thank you for teaching me to use both!

ONE

I am six years old, and I am SO pissed. Mom took away my stuffies (what I called my stuffed animals), because I talk to them too much. Yeah, DUH, it would be rude not to return polite conversation.

So, when the quack Doctor told her to take them away, yeah, the conversations stopped. I had no friends left and I sat in my room for years drawing superhero's that are just stick figures and reading fantasy novels instead. Real healthy Doc, thanks a LOT.

Somehow, when they asked me if I "REALLY" hear the stuffed animals talking, my answer, which was, "Don't you?" caused them to suggest I may have a disorder.

That was 1999.

Turns out, I have a dissociative personality. I don't lose time or become someone else exactly, but I did have some years where some cool people lived in my head with me. They sort of talked to me through other objects, like, say, stuffed animals.

They didn't tell me to burn shit or anything like that but, they were my friends and I missed them for years. And then, I stopped taking my meds in 2010. A couple days later, BAM, the band was back together.

Arvind, the smartest person (or stuffed animal) you could ever meet, came back to me one day as my *Clayton Kershaw* bobble head. He greeted me and was happy to see me. I was shocked, scared, and happy all at once. I cried. I REALLY did. It was not until later that same week when Andrea and Roku also came to visit in the form of my Tick and Arthur action figures.

(Look, if you don't know who the Tick and Arthur are, you don't *deserve to* know. Shame, shame on you.)

That was in my very late teen years.

My besties are all unique. As I would get to know them over the years, the special traits each of them had would become clear. Andrea is an amazing code breaker, puzzle solver. She can literally destroy any magazine crossword puzzle in a minute, whereas Roku has this over-active sense of empathy and awareness. He was always the first to comfort me when I was a child. I think I missed him most during those years of medication and boredom. Of course, I already said that Arvind is the smartest person I know. That is a total understatement by the way!

I'm John. John Thomas Fitch. I am a cop and I live in the central coast of California. A *"totally bitchin"* town called "Vista Tranquila." This means, "Quiet View" in English, due to the lack of noise, roads, and the serene ocean we are nestled up to.

It's all about surf and wine tasting around here. I do neither.

I am the template for an average Caucasian man. I'm roughly five foot ten inches tall, and I weight roughly 180lbs. Most of that is a mix of junk food, whatever muscle I can create by doing ten push-ups a night, well, OK, three times a week anyways and I have a lovely head of puffy brown hair. I have a receding hairline that I call a FIVE-head, as it takes five fingers to touch hair if I line my hand to my brow. I wear decent clothes, if not expensive, certainly not cheap, but I wrap the garbage as best I can in mid-grade style. I am awkward and insane.

About the only interesting this about me is the fact I am an orphan. Both my parents became lost at sea when I was young.

It is assumed that the sailboat they were on, somewhere near Norway, must have capsized in rough weather. The boat and the six passengers were never found. I carry an old picture of them in my padfolio. An old Polaroid of the six doomed passengers right before they left on the trip. My dad loved using old Polaroids, even after the film was hard to find.

Don't worry, I was crazy BEFORE that happened.

Any questions?

I am a cop. I made detective a few months back. I am one of three we have in this entire region. I feel pretty lucky to have passed the criteria to even be on the police force based on my childhood history. But "officially" that was WAY back when I was a young kid. I got lucky to be in a small town.

Regarding being a detective, truth is, no one else wanted the job. Not much to do.

My issue is that I am not a great detective. I am VERY detail oriented and write SUPER clean reports, I just don't solve much. I mainly log complaints, do a bunch of follow up and occasionally find some stolen items.

It's honest work, but I have ZERO instincts. Stuff you cannot teach.

The other two detectives are seasoned pros and do the big stuff. Detective Raines is nearing retirement and many of us wonder if he can find a way to relax and do nothing. He is intense, in an awesome older guy sort of way. Rumor is that he has a six-pack under that suit, and he is over SIXTY!

Kari Skarsgard is a handsome woman with a very calming and pleasing disposition. She is the one that gets people to spill stuff they did before they KNEW they spilled it! At least that is what I hear. I have yet to observe her doing her magic. I think it is the charm she emits due to her slight accent, which sounds to me to be Norwegian. I mean, DUH, "Skarsgard" right! She is also a huge wine enthusiast and knows everyone in this region, or so she says. I think she will make a great mayor someday if half of what she says is true about her knowledge of the area.

Once I got into the force, I had to make sure no funny stuff happened. Meaning, imaginary friends had to go away. As I reached my mid-twenties, it had been years since I heard from them. It was easier to deal with the isolation as an adult as compared to a lonely kid.

Our Monday routine in our small police station is to have a morning briefing, watch Skarsgard put away a maple-bar in three wolfing bites and sort of go over our open task list and do a divide and conquer approach to the week.

I figure Skarsgard is about 38. Not quite 40, but not mid-thirties either. I'd say about 6 years older than I am. I spend too much time wondering if younger guys are her type. I wonder if she even has a type. She literally never talks about personal stuff and never has a date to the wine events. I try to stalk her social media posts and can't find anything. I mean, NO SOCIAL MEDIA AT ALL! It baffles me to the point of obsession how private she is, and how a 60-YEAR-OLD has a SIX PACK! Again, I am a crap detective.

We have an awesome Salt-Water fish tank in the main bullpen that was donated by the local Chamber of Commerce. One of my primary duties is to feed the three fish that reside in the tank twice a day. The crab gets whatever is on the bottom. Kind of like me.

Donuts, CHECK, Fish, CHECK, File, catalog and generate reports, W-I-P.

Yup, just me laying down the law. Yawn.

When something big happens in the "V-T" everyone knows it. Vista Tranquila is too small a community for anything to go unnoticed. Husbands don't cheat on wives, unless they are itching to be caught, Wives don't flirt with the pool-boy and kids don't usually step too far out of line. It's just our thing. Being steady but unspectacular. So, when a young woman's body was found last week. It was major news and very disruptive.

Young woman, in her twenties, sandy blonde hair was found lying in a coastal hillside amongst the tall grass in a meadow area. Local livestock roam and feed in these areas and the staff tending them found her. No signs of injury, she was just lying there dead.

We will know more when the autopsy report comes back, but nothing obvious. Consider that we have no real throughfare and usually bodies are dropped off nearer to a major highway so, it's not clear that this is a "dead drop".

The active theory around here is MAYBE a "Spring Waver" come into town and had an overdose. Dropped here by the others at the "party." It makes it local foul play but not aggravated assault or murder.

When the *Spring Wave*, as we call it, comes once a year, we get a lot of non-locals come to look at the California Poppies and have some down-time in our beachfront village. It is small but has great food, drinks and wine tasting for a weekend.

We ride the Spring Wave as a local commerce boost and welcome it. Usually, the arrests go up some due to DUI's and public disturbances of the youngsters cutting loose a bit.

Regarding the body, I keep telling myself to stop waiting on Raines to weigh in his own theory, but he has not budged much. I just can't help but to be curious what HE thinks. He is the one I bet will come closest to finding the real story arc. I am trying to develop an active theory, but nothing is coming to me beyond an overdose. We will get the autopsy report any day to provide more detail.

While I am musing this over, I randomly begin to wonder if Skarsgard has seen Raines six-pack. She is the one that told me he has one…I think. If she saw it, maybe THEY are secretly seeing one another romantically (even though he could be her father).

I stop myself and remind my DETAIL oriented brain to FOCUS. I need to pay attention. Captain is about to grill us about the crime scene and our working theory, which, (by the way) was all chronicled by ME. See, the details are MY thing. I submitted a Pulitzer worthy report just last night. Skarsgard even said so before inhaling the donut. Five pages of just about nothing. Woman. Dead. Blonde. Nonlocal. Fingerprint ID had her living in Northern California nearer to San Francisco.

Our captain is named Juniper Bradley. She is an African American woman that is the true class of the department. She is tough, fair and a true salt of the earth person. As she enters our little area, she looks upset. She looks at Raines and says:

"Another body. Another young woman. Just found."

She then turns to look our way to make sure we heard and goes back to looking at Raines.

"Otter watchers found her in the rocks off the beach about twenty minutes ago. I need you guys to process the scene immediately as this is going to inflame the locals and we obviously may have a bigger problem if these two events are connected." She pauses before continuing, "We have two detectives, you guys go detect something to help get this thing in order" looking toward Raines and back toward Skarsgard (Who is standing right next to me, HELLO!).

I hate that because I am new, I don't get treated as a serious Detective, more like a clerk or admin. Two detectives my ass. I passed the TEST!

Raines, already standing, regards Captain Bradley with a serious face that looks as if it was made of stone.

"If the two bodies connect, we are going to get immediately overrun by outside help, likely FBI. That is not to mention the locals going into panic."

Raines grabs his coat and keys and says:

"Let's try and get ahead of it. If we can eliminate any form of continuity here, we can give you something to put in your afternoon statement."

He looks at me and motions me to follow.

"Let's go Birdy. We need you to catalogue while we have a closer look."

I HATE when he calls me that. He used to think my name was "FINCH," instead of Fitch. Then he started calling me "Birdy." The Birdy tag stuck.

Whatever, he has a six-pack at sixty. I guess he gets to make shit-up if he wants to.

As I grab my padfolio, my eyes lock onto the fish tank. I can't help but notice the puffer fish is giving me an odd look. I turn to get out of Skarsgard's path and look back to find the puffer, the blue fish (like the one played by the comedian gal in that cartoon about the lost clown fish) and the white angel fish ALL seem to be staring at me.

I am transfixed for a moment, but Raines calls out for me to "grab waders from the gear locker," breaking my daze. We will be near water so, makes sense.

I grab the boots, my camera equipment and off to the rocky coast the four of us go.

Two

Nothing obvious at the accident scene. We are careful not to call it a "crime" scene until we know it is. The woman, whom we figure is in her mid-twenties, is surely dead, but no obvious signs of trauma. She is just laying amongst the craggy rocks.

Squirrels dominate this area of the coastal front. The Otters continue to form a raft of little furry bodies about 50-feet off the shore, floating on their backs enjoying the day.

The family that found the woman is traumatized, as they should be, but mainly the late teens girl seems the most distraught. Seems unfair. You come to the coast to take in some ocean air and watch the otters and have the stroke of luck to have a life changing experience. And not in a good way.

All materials are noted, which is not much and most of it I muse will be trash that was here already. The area leading to the craggy beach is impossible to process as so many people have already walked up and down the pathway. I do my best.

I stand at the top of the bank looking down at Skarsgard and Raines as they finish up. Something is gnawing at me. Something about the body and the environment. I can't help but make a few extra notes as I tap into my own observations.

How does a body lay so elegantly in an area which, had you fallen or fainted, would have resulted in a more disheveled laying profile? Sharp rocks would have caused an uneven fall and the way the body lay would not be peacefully nestled. Further, anyone falling down here would have been cut by the shore rocks. It would be like doing a bellyflop into broken glass and not having a cut.

This body was placed here. But, for now, I keep my own theory to myself.

I take some photos of the surroundings and make extra sure to actively try and get PEOPLE in the shots without it being obvious. I have seen to many movies where the culprit is lurking at the back of the crowd gathered at a crime scene.

Skarsgard approaches me and motions for me to follow her.

"I'm done here John," she says. "We need to go over both reports and visual documentation before giving Captain Bradley the details." She regards my camera, "Did you get everything you need? All the angles and the nearby nooks?"

I confirm as I begin to walk to the SUV. I see Captain Bradley talking to Raines and wonder if he is already telling her his findings. Is this whole report and write-up just ceremony? Does the senior sleuth have the scent?

I shake it off and head back with Skarsgard. My report will take up the rest of my day, and I am fighting back the words about my own theory. I am not sure why. Maybe I am afraid of looking stupider than I already do to Skarsgard or maybe it's something else. I end up saying nothing to her and she says little as we exit the coastal area.

Suddenly she fixes her penetrating eyes on me and profoundly blurts:

"It's a serial event John. I fucking know it."

Stunned by her random eruption of speculation I can't help but to try and get her to probe deeper.

"We may be able to link these two deaths when we get all of the data together and the autopsy details, but what makes you feel that way based on what we found today?" I reply.

She shakes her head and stares straight forward as I guide the SUV back to the station.

"I don't know. It is just that both scenes are extremely clean. Too clean and the profile of the deceased are very similar." She says. "But there is nothing obvious...which is why my instincts are telling me THAT is the clue in itself."

Not bad, I think to myself, I can kind of groove to that logic. But, again, I say nothing of my own thoughts.

When night falls, Raines grabs his keys and rinses his coffee mug in the sink area near the endless sea of coffee pods and creamers. Yeah, we all LOVE coffee and drink it sweet. His mug has a picture of a young female child on it and reads: "Cammie loves Pop-Pop." A gift from his granddaughter.

He squeezes his temples before he knuckles the table near Skarsgard and seemingly addresses us both:

"Have a nice evening, be *careful*, and be here early. Two dead females is something to keep in mind, but we have got to get ahead of this if it goes overly public yeah?"

I note that he seems very irritable, almost nervous.

Skarsgard looks up at him, nods acknowledgement while he fixes his eyes on me before he turns to leave.

I make a note that his lack of eye contact with Skarsgard may imply he is worried about her and trying not to show it! It sure was not for me, and that implies two key things:

One, that he CARES.

Hmph!

And two, that he is not ruling out foul play here. YES, I am starting to think like a detective!

Suddenly, I am annoyed. I snap off my own comment as he leaves:

"Enjoy your sit-ups and crunches" I say.

After the comment comes out, I cringe. Why the hell did I say that!

Raines looks back at me with a wholly perplexed look and almost seems hurt by my rude jab.

"Uh, OK Birdy" he says awkwardly, "You, uh, have a nice evening." He says.

He turns with a kind of "What the hell was that" look on his face and exits our bullpen.

Skarsgard seems about to laugh as she watches Raines leave and gives me a short look but fully ignores me and my comment for the rest of the evening.

As she begins gathering her own things, preparing to leave, I awkwardly blurt:

"Got plans tonight?"

She looks at me only for a second and heads for the door. She shouts over her shoulder:

"Sit-ups and crunches John. That's what we all do every night isn't it"

I cringe and decide to just sit quietly and sulk. I get it. I know what is happening. I have a damn schoolboys crush on Skarsgard and now I am acting like an idiot. Aaaaaagh. I don't want to have a crush and I am shit with people. Especially when I need to be charming and full of allure.

I feel sort of sick.

I decide to dive into the two reports and the photos I took of both dead women. I agree, this is connected, but need more than what I have currently to take THAT leap with either of the "real" detectives or captain Bradley.

As the evening progresses, the station empties, and I find myself alone with the only light being our bullpen area, the saltwater fish tank, and the dim hallways for the cleaning crew. I go over and over the detail of the cases and realize it is useless. There is nothing there.

I feel like I am being watched and I turn to find the three fish staring at me again. I realize I have not fed them, and I drop a few crumbles of food into the tank before I sit back down.

As I sit, I am surprised to hear a familiar voice from behind me.

I leap upright and spin to face the sound. It came from…
THE FISH TANK!

"Hi John, mind if I have a look at your file. Might be able to help you find a pattern or something else that is relevant," Andrea's voice fills my ears. A voice I have not heard in over 13 years. A voice that brings me so much joy.

I stare in shock as the blue fish swims to the front of the glass and stares at me expectantly.

I realize immediately that this is an awfully bad thing. I bury my head in my hands quickly accepting what this means.

I sit quietly, considering my situation. After a few minutes I start to pile up my file papers and photos. Resigned to the fact that I am nuts, I just go with it.

I shake my head and ask myself *"what am I DOING?"* as I walk over and start to reveal case details to the…fish!

I mean DUH, this is Andrea after all. If anyone can find linkage, it's her.

THREE

Andrea swims back and forth as she peruses the pages I am holding up to the glass of the tank. Every now and again she urges me onward to the next page with a comment like, "next," or "please continue." I reach the end of the documentation I have, including the pictures taken thus far of the two victims.

She slows the pace of her side-to-side swimming and peers around the last page saying:

"I am done John. Thank you for your patience."

As I put the papers back into the file folders and document carrier, I am sort of at a loss for how to proceed with Andrea, the FISH version. Before I can blurt something nonsensical, she beats me to it.

"I think we need to continue this when we get the autopsy reports. As of now, these two deaths share little more than gender and general location vicinity, if you consider the space between the hillside and the rocky coastline within a reasonable vicinity."

So even the great mind of the code-breaking Andrea cannot find linkage here. I am right where I was BEFORE I started to have delusions again. Great.

I look at her blue-fishy form and decide to catch-up a bit with her. She is, after all, one of my oldest friends. I sit next to the fish tank, and we have a short chat about any number of things that are only somewhat interesting.

After a while, as we wind down, the puffer fish swims over to the vicinity of Andrea and begins to address us:

"Have you considered that the LACK of linkage, may in fact be the linkage in and of itself? The pure lack of anything makes this interestingly similar and I think that is the link". Says the voice of Arvind.

Arvind has always been the smartest person, er, fish I know. Not surprised to find out that he is here in the fish-tank also.

I nod, while not really feeling like we have anything to work from. I say:

"I think that is the same logic Skarsgard has Arvind."

I look around the tank briefly and ask:

"Arvind, if you are here and Andrea is here, then…."

I look at the white angel fish that is hanging out near the bottom right-hand side of the aquarium and ask:

"Roku?

The Angel fish swims over and aggressively flippers back and forth in front of me.

"Hi John. Yes, I am here also, all four of us are here to help you."

Excellent, so the gang is all here, and the caper is afoot, as they say.

Wait, FOUR?

I look at the only other aquarium occupant, which is a small crab, and ask, "Who is he?" pointing to the crab.

The fish just stare at me with no response. I figure if I have a new dissociative pal, it will talk to me at some point, when I need its expertise.

HEY, maybe the crab is a martial artist. GREAT!

Getting right back to business Arvind bumps against the glass a few times and begins to ask questions that I feel like I have already covered.

"When they do the autopsy, will they for sure dust the body for prints John?

Before waiting for an answer, he continues:

"Also, and more importantly, can you pull together all the crowd photos of the crime scenes for me. The aftermath gatherings and such?"

I nod my head profusely and realize that Arvind is on the same track I was that the "Hollywood" style killer likes to see the "fuss" by showing up when police are processing the crime scene.

I pull the crowd photos out of the file and begin looking at them myself.

"Ahem..." says Arvind.

I look up at him and realize, he is waiting.

"Sorry. I just wanted to take one last look" I say.

I begin to show the pics to all three fish. The crab seems indifferent. It's really hard to tell with those crab eyes.

Both crime scenes have varying amounts of people near them. The beach area is far more populated with onlookers than the hillside meadow.

The hillside body was found quite a bit later, based on the estimated time of death, as compared to the beach body. In fact, the hillside shows only the hillside workers (three men) and the authorities processing the scene. Little else.

I jump ahead to show the fish how smart I am by stating the obvious.

"The three hillside workers are not in any of the beach crime scenes. That means we are not going to find any onlookers at the hillside that match up to the beach scene."

Andrea, moving suddenly in an erratic pattern seems about to burst as she moves closer to the tanks glass.

"I see a pattern. And I think it may be relevant." She pauses for effect, "There is one thing here that is slightly out of place. It is circumstantial at best, but it is a pattern."

The other two fish and I seem to hold our breath as we wait for the great reveal.

See, that is funny, FISH holding their breath!

Andrea continues:

"The one public servant at both scenes that really does NOT have to be there is in three different photos. The park ranger."

I turn the photos back toward myself and begin to look closer and find what Andrea is referencing. Tommy Abel, one of the local park rangers is clearly found at both scenes. The tall dark-haired man, roughly forty years old or so, is generally a nice guy, always helpful.

I shake my head to minimize the finding.

"That's just Tommy. It is not so far-fetched that he would be at these scenes doing crowd control or whatever else rangers do."

Roku swims forward and asks for me to turn specific beach pictures toward the glass. He wants to see everything with the late teens girl that found the beach body.

Roku stops me on a specific photo.

"There. That one."

Andrea, Arvind, and I begin to study the picture. I see nothing of note with the exception being that Tommy is in the photo as well.

Roku continues.

"Look at the ranger, Tommy. Look at how he is looking at the girl."

As I look closer, based on this single frame of time, it seems that the park ranger is fixated on the girl.

I know Tommy a little. He also spends some of his free time as a wine tasting host for one of the local wineries. He is one of those guys that spends his days on the job and his evenings and open weekend days mixing with the local wine enthusiasts doing pouring events.

Roku swims away still talking.

"From a perspective of this single photo, his gaze looks fixated on the girl. It's not evidence, but it helps us create an emotional narrative here. I suggest we bookmark the ranger and pay close attention to him going forward."

I can't stop staring at the photo. The tall dark-haired man does look a bit odd, almost creepy in how he is leering at the girl.

Just like that, the four of us spring a plan to look deeper into our newly formed narrative.

Time for a beach day on the coast for a closer look at Tommy.

The next day I get to the station early. I am eagerly waiting for Skarsgard to arrive so I can bring her up to speed a bit on my latest line of thinking.

Raines is the first to arrive.

As he sits down at his desk, he looks at me intently. I act like I don't see him, but he is not buying it. He walks over to stand next to me.

"Out with-it Birdy."

I look up at him as if I am confused by his statement.

He levels a glare at me as he continues.

"What's eating you and why are my stomach muscles on your mind?"

He patiently, but sternly continues to stare at me.

Suddenly I feel ridiculous about my attitude, my whole line of thinking about he and Skarsgard and the fact that I am even remotely jealous.

I decide to fall on the sword. If I don't, he will just do his Jedi-mind-trick on me anyways. This is Raines we are talking about.

"I am sorry detective. I was acting like an idiot" I am kind of dealing with a small personal crisis. I did not mean to act disrespectfully to you."

The older man regards me calmly, almost fatherly and leans against my desk while crossing his arms.

"You know Birdy, women can be a challenge, but there is not a one of us guys that would be here without our best gals. That includes both moms and wives." He looks at me sympathetically. I feel my cheeks start to burn pink. He thinks I have a romance problem. Wow, very fatherly of him.

"Don't be shocked or ashamed man. I am a detective. It's OK. Do yourself a favor, work it out with the gal, whomever she is." As he says that, a gal named Mona Gallo from the crime lab walks into the station followed closely by Skarsgard.

He unfolds his arms and places a hand on my right shoulder as he continues.

"Remember, it is NEVER a good idea to shit where you eat"

He says this while looking straight at the two women as they enter.

He winks at me and begins to walk away. Stopping suddenly, he looks back at me, as if conflicted in speaking his next words.

"Anyways kid, a word of advice in case you ever father a girl, boys are *speedbumps* on the road to success. Don't forget that and make your daughter wait to date idiots like us until she is 25 years old".

Skarsgard hears that last part as she puts down her purse and keys and says,

"Amen detective Raines"

He ignores her as he walks away, but I swear I see him smiling.

I stare at the fish tank with a *"what the hell did that mean?"* kind of look. All three fish are staring at Raines. Roku seems to agree. Not sure how I got THAT from looking at a fish but, he really does.

Raines grabs his notebook and pen as he heads to the morning briefing area.

I am half stunned by the exchange as I stare blanky at the wall. I realize that if Raines figured I have a crush, (and he stared RIGHT at Skarsgard), then she probably also knows. They are detectives for fucks sake.

I look at the fish and bury my face is my hands.

"FUCK!"

Four

When Skarsgard comes over to talk to me, I can't seem to look at her. In fact, my whole plan for the day is shot.

I NEED to FOCUS!

I can hear the fish talking to me from the tank as Arvind shouts:

"Eye on the prize John. Now more than ever, right?"

I ignore him and continue to listen as Raines walks through his updates and plans for next steps.

Seems the autopsy reports are being delivered sometime in the late morning today. That will be good data for me and the fish to peruse as we refocus my mind. With that, I move ahead with my initial plan.

I look at both Detectives and decide to lay out my own plans for the day.

"I want to walk the beach scene and general vicinity again. I also want to talk to a few of the scene processing folks and get some clarifications for my notes."

I see that Raines is about to ask me for more detail and decide to cut him short.

"I don't have anything in the way of theory, but I feel like my notes are a bit lacking. I think a few folks can recall enough minor detail to help me fluff it a bit" I lie.

The trick is to not implicate Tommy as a person of interest until it has some validity. These guys already think of me as a third wheel so, no need to blunder a legitimate shot at finding a thread to pull.

When the reports arrive, we wait like vultures to go over the findings. I go for the smart play and let Raines and Skarsgard peruse the files first. She is so impatient she can't even wait and just looks over his shoulder the whole time. He does not seem to mind. I listen to them to hear if they discuss the findings, but it's mainly Raines mumbling almost as if to himself. Then he starts to address us more clearly with his thoughts as he keeps poking through the file.

Turns out both dead women have traceable amounts of the same substances in their blood. Flunitrazepam, Gamma Hydroxybutyric Acid (GHB) and Ketamine.

Alone these substances aren't exactly commonly ingested, but in a cocktail together they are well known to cause a sleepwalking affect. People tend to lose reasoning and usually have zero recall of events that took place while they were dosed with this.

Raines is the first to call it what it is.

"So, someone gave these gals a *good-night Cinderella*."

Skarsgard seems to already know what this is, and thanks to the narration I am receiving from Arvind, I am getting a real time explanation. In short, these deaths just became official homicides.

Raines continues to explain.

"This is mostly used in Brazil, especially on the populated beaches like Copacabana and the like. Scammers and thieves will drop this mix into a person's drink. Once they see it take effect, they will get you back to your own hotel room and rob you blind, or worse! Once you are already a few drinks in, you likely won't even realize you aren't working with your full faculties in place".

The two detectives continue to process the information on the report. In both cases the cause of death is a stroke, which is usually caused by a lack of blood flow to the brain.

So, two deaths, two drug induced Zombies that both die of stroke.

The report also identifies multiple fingerprints throughout the bodies of the victims. Something to work with anyways.

I wait until the two other detectives are done and begin to start their next actions and I grab the reports for myself (and my fish). I sit with my back to the fish tank so they can also have a look.

Nothing unusual beyond what the others found and noted.

Andrea is particularly interested in the fingerprints and the photos with locations of the prints. She makes me stay on these a little longer than other documents.

She stops her review and tells us she has the first viable clue. Being the codebreaker and pattern finding genius, I am not surprised at the least.

She references one particular fingerprint, which is a partial print.

"Look at the print on the 3rd page notation. Look at where it is located. It seems to me that even as a partial it is the size of a thumb. That is relevant!" she says.

Our break is on the hillside victim. A partial fingerprint located in the neck region on the carotid artery. The artery which when pressed will stop blood flow to the brain, usually resulting in losing consciousness and if still blocked thereafter, stroke!

I look at the fish and consider my next steps over again. A plan begins to form in my mind. I bend down as I whisper to my dissociative fish friends,

"Guys, lets hold off on the coastal beach day. I think I feel like doing some wine tasting instead"

The weekend can't come fast enough as I firm up my plan. The initial idea to create a random meeting with Tommy while he is on duty would have created too many update issues with Raines. As I update my notes, he would have expected something of use. So, I delay that with menial tasks on other cases.

The weekends in Vista Tranquila are usually dominated by coastal shopping in the quaint commerce areas and wine tasting at local winery locations scattered throughout the region. The younger crowd usually heads to the Alleyway, which is a series of six or so tasting room locations that funnel into a few small restaurants and eateries. The Alleyway creates a sort of charm based on its polar opposite architecture to the surrounding area. It is built out of an old industrial complex that has been shut down for over a decade. The local Chamber of Commerce President had the stroke of brilliance to convert the area into a kind of industrial outside, warm inside, series of cozy tasting rooms and evening mingle locations. One of these tasting rooms pours the juice from a local wine maker called Onyx Mountain, named for the dark rocky hillside located in the view of the winery.

Onyx is where Tommy spends his evenings and some weekends pouring and mingling with wine enthusiasts.

As I enter Onyx's tasting room, I see the draw for folks to use this as a sort of hang-out. The inside is totally redone, and all the industrial piping is painted and made to kind of develop a hi-tech look and feel that is in total contrast to the large couches, cozy seating areas, tables full of board games and high-top tables for smaller groups. The place smells like lavender. Very cozy.

I see Tommy standing behind an area that is not exactly a bar, but more of a functional pouring area. He does not notice me. There is a balding, middle aged, bear of a man with an overly jolly look to him standing near a table loaded with what looks like cupcakes to his left. A red-head gal whom I have never met greets me and asks me if I am here to taste. I confirm that I am and ask if I can use one of the high-top tables. I pull my phone out and play a video of the fish tank that I took at Arvind's request. As the fish appear on the video, my dissociative disorder takes over and I can interact with the fish in real time. Remember, it's all in my head anyways. Man, I am a messed-up dude.

Roku speaks to me first.

"The plan is to get a tasting with Tommy so we can get a glass with a print without obviously stealing the glass. You need to go to the counter and taste with Tommy, not the Redhead John."

I nod my head as I keep the phone open and video looping in my lap.

"I know Roku. I am waiting for someone."

The fish don't congregate but keep swimming in the formations and movements they did when I took the video. Andrea's voice chimes in,

"Good idea. Don't want to be caught here alone being creepy. But you don't have any friends John, except for us". She says laughingly.

I laugh at the poke and restart the video.

"I invited the gal from forensics. Mona Gallo. She always seems interested in hanging out, so I thought this was a good time to take her up on it."

Arvind laughs and Roku chimes in again,

"Yes, she is a little interested in you, in my opinion. Maybe a bit more curious about you, but it's a good call John".

Coming from my emotionally intelligent fish-friend, that is high praise. Maybe she likes me. I kind of like her in an oddly different way than I like Skarsgard.

I nod and shut the video down. Remember, *"shitting where you eat"*, bad!

Mona Gallo, one of our forensic technicians enters and sees me sitting at the high-top and waves at me. She sits and we spend a few minutes in conversation. I suck at small talk.

The redhead comes over to us and asks us if we want to do a tasting flight of some reds they are pouring or if we have something else in mind. Before Mona can speak, I suggest we go to the counter and taste there, motioning over to Tommy.

The redhead smiles and walks us over. She points out the cupcake counter and Mona seems excited about those. Maybe even more than the wine. She drags me in front of the baked goods table before we get seated at the tasting counter.

She smiles at the large red cheeked balding man and rises up on her tippy toes while voicing her inquiry in a high pitch,

"What do you have here?" She asks excitedly.

The man chuckles and seems extremely excited to tell her all about his varying flavors of cupcake. Each meant to be paired with a specific wine. Mona squeals with excitement and starts picking out cupcakes. The man, very eager to please, hands her a "palate cleaning" glass of water out of a filtered faucet at the side of the counter and hands her the box of sweets.

"Glass of water for you. Really clears the palate for the wine and cupcakes. And the cakes will be added to your tasting tab."

Mona laughs,

"We haven't even started yet so no thank you!"

The man nods and motions us to head to the counter,

"Come back and tell me what you think. Or better yet, give me an online review, BUT only if its positive." He laughs enthusiastically as he hands Mona his card.

She looks at it and reads it aloud,

"Drunken Cakes by Drew." She says.

He smiles and continues to chuckle his belly laugh as he says,

"That's me, Drew Booth, the Cupcake King!"

Mona laughs, hauls me and her box of cupcakes to the counter for our tasting.

As we settle in at the tasting counter, I take a quick look around the tasting room.

Mona and I, along with three younger women are at the tasting counter. Drew, the happy cupcake king is at his table loading up replacement cupcakes for what Mona bought. Tommy is behind the tasting counter serving the three gals, the red headed host is standing by the door tidying branded t-shirts and two men are seated at the couches talking and drinking a bottle of wine.

Tommy sees us and finishes pouring for the group of younger gals before he comes over and says hello.

"Hey John, Mona. Great to see you." He looks at us both and I begin to fight the urge to open the video again and bring the fish in straightaway. I can tell by his *smirk* that he is wondering if Mona and I are here together.

We have some more polite conversation and I order us a tasting of the reds they are pouring. $20 for four pours. I wonder if this is a good price. I don't know ANYTHING about wine.

As I sip my first glass, I can't help but observe Tommy as he flirts relentlessly with the more buxom of the three young women. This guy is not even hiding his interest.

He is obviously a total player, but he is also so, how can I describe it, *smarmy*. It's pretty annoying.

Mona seems OK with my limited interest in conversing as she enjoys her wine and the limited conversation I offer. She does notice I am hardly touching my first glass.

"Don't like the Merlot?" She asks.

I look at her and then my wine glass, which is still half full before I respond.

"It's lovely. It just gives me the worst heartburn." I say while smiling.

She laughs and digs into her small clutch type of purse, pulling out a small pill bottle.

"Here" she says, handing me a small tablet. "Take this. It will help."

I shrug and mindlessly take the pill.

My attention, however, is on Tommy the whole time. I notice that he never actually touches our glass as he pours our tastings. Initially he picked up the glasses with the crux webbing area between his pointer and middle fingers as he placed them in front of us. I doubt I have a useable print.

I do however notice he is holding the wine bottle.

After about an hour, and our tastings are finished, Mona heads to the restroom and I can't help it and open my phone and play the video.

Arvind hurriedly speaks.

"John, not much time. Listen closely. The bottle of Zinfandel is almost done. Order a glass and when he drains the bottle ask him for it. Tell him you are going to have it cut into a candle."

I shake my head confused.

"What? What the fuck does that mean?" I whisper.

Arvind tells me to look behind me, on the wall. I see a poster that advertises a local craft shop will cut bottles and fill them with wax and make them into a decorative candle.

I nod agreement and realize Mona is nearly back, as she exits the restroom. I close the video down and put my phone away.

I offer to buy her a glass of wine and she accepts. I suggest the Zinfandel, but unfortunately, she says she prefers Pinot Noir.

Looks like I am getting Zinfandel.

The plan works perfectly as we drain the Zinfandel bottle. Tommy has no problem with me taking the bottle to turn into a candle, even though he laughs at me. The nerve of this dickhead.

"It's actually *not* one of our more attractive bottles John" he says.

I notice he texts something to the gal he had been pouring for, openly without any subterfuge whatsoever.

Just then, I hear a voice behind me that I recognize. Skarsgard walks up to Mona and me.

"What's this? John Fitch having a life!" She says with a laugh as she greets Mona. I realize it's more of a jab than a real question. I play along and offer her my stool. She refuses and continues to stand.

She points at my padfolio and says, "Always ready to take notes eh John!"

I laugh. I had not even realized I had it with me. It comes far too naturally.

Tommy is too wrapped up in the young women and does not offer to pour anything for Skarsgard. I call out to him to get her a glass. She waves me off.

"I am fine John. Thank you though. I have some friends outside anyways. You know this is my thing!", she says offhandedly.

I don't even realize that I had pulled my phone out and the video is playing.

Mona looks at my phone and comments,

"Are those the fish from the station?"

It startles me and I move to close the video. Before I can, Roku yells at me,

"John, don't. Just say you use it as a screen saver or something. Don't put us away".

I follow his advice and it seems to satisfy both the ladies I am with.

Just then, Tommy brings me my bottle and asks if we want anything else. He wants us to close out. He is pretty distracted.

As he places the bottle on the counter, full of beautiful newly added fingerprints of his own, he actually FLIRTS with Mona right in front of both Skarsgard and I! I cannot get over what a player this guy is. He then drops the check onto the counter with a wink.

I grab the check, as Mona protests, and give her a wink of my own that makes Skarsgard laugh out loud.

"Wow John, you are a real smoothy," she jabs at me.

Both ladies have a laugh at my expense, even if Mona's is more of a flirty giggle. Skarsgard heads back to where I assume her friends are gathered, and Mona and I begin to leave.

As I am walking out, Mona looks down at me holding the bottle.

"You going to swipe that napkin?"

I realize I am holding the bottle with a napkin around it (to not add my prints). I am also hoping I don't wipe off Tommy's prints. I look at Mona and realize this must look odd.

I decide to leave it alone, give her a shrug and just let her think what she wants. The next step will be to ask her for some forensic help, so, at some point I will need to bring her into the loop, I just hope she is not offended when I do.

FIVE

I place the wine bottle in my desk drawer at the station. I have decided not to pull the prints off of it myself. I will want Mona to do that. Then, finesse her to do a forensic comparison of the prints she pulls versus the partial we have in the case file.

I am itching to get through our morning meetings and captain Bradley even makes a joke at how distracted I seem. Whatever. I wait until we are through it, I gather the case file, with a focus on being subtle, and I follow Roku's suggestions on how to approach Mona.

Roughly thirty minutes before noon, I head over to Mona's lab area and go to work. Armed with Roku on screen, two BBQ chicken salads I picked up from a local café, as a gesture to soften the request, I take the plunge.

As I enter with a knock, she looks up at me and seems to brighten. I hold up the two salads with an inquisitive gesture and she smiles and claps excitedly.

So far so good.

As we are eating, she and I discuss the weekend and the wine tasting. She pledges to take me to an even better winery next time. Noted. Roku is now laughing out loud about how I might have a girlfriend if I "manage to not screw it up".

Mona asks me about how distracted I seemed. She notes specifically that I seemed like I was elsewhere and my tendency to mumble to myself. Great, so now I know that I am mumbling to the fish aloud, and other people are seeing it.

She sees my discomfort and offers me a reassurance that it is OK.

"Don't worry. I still had a nice time. Babbling to yourself is one of my favorite things to do, just, maybe, get out of your phone a little more."

Well, OK. Since babbling to non-existent friends is OK with her, she just might be someone I can spend a little time with.

I decide to stop stalling and I lay the whole scenario out for Mona. From being sensitive to looking like an idiot to the senior officers and to being careful not to accuse Tommy unjustly, thus the reasons for secrecy.

I tell her my NOT-so-subtle strategy for the prints, which she was on-hand to witness, and I hastily conclude:

"And that is why I was holding the bottle with a napkin."

She looks down at her salad and continues to eat while not looking at me. Roku tells me to just sit quietly and NOT do ANYTHING!

After a few bites she says:

"Ok, so, you want prints taken off the bottle. Your primary suspect is the cutie Ranger from the tasting room, and this is all below board. Right?"

I acknowledge and clarify it is MY active thread I am chasing. Not anyone else's.

She stops eating and looks at me with a hard stare before her lips start to form a hint of a smile.

"I want a week of salads just like this one, an upper shoulder and neck rub in private (She points to the back of her neck), and for us to go to MY favorite tasting room EVEN THOUGH I was a pawn in your mysterious detective game John!". She looks back down again and keeps eating before she continues,

"When you really get to know me, you will fall for me. I may be a geek and I am not a brand everyone goes for, BUT you will miss me when I'm gone pal", she says with a wink of her own.

Roku tells me that her feelings are slightly hurt in his opinion. But she is openly flirting with me through it. That's good, right?

How she handled this makes me like her even more. Roku jabbering is like having my own private shrink in my pocket. He chirps his analysis at me the whole time.

Mona raises her right arm to me and opens her palm out facing upwards.

"Bottle, before I change my mind and request a foot rub also!"

I run back to my desk and grab the case file and the bottle and hustle back to Mona's lab. I show her the case file and the 3rd page photo with the partial print notated on it. She finds the print imaged in the computers forensic report and begins to process the bottle. She pulls twelve prints off the bottle when all is finished. As expected, all of them belong to employees of the winery or the tasting room.

Now the magic happens. She takes a digital portion of Tommy's print that would mate up to the partial on the artery on page 3. She cuts exactly what she would need, as all the prints are now imaged in her lab software. As the prints pull together and she does not get a positive result. She mumbles to me as she reopens the file,

"I was trying to be cute by matching partial to partial. Let's just overlay all the prints on the same angle and see what pops".

She rotates each print, laying them on top of the partial from the file.

She shoves her chair backwards and throws her arms in the air triumphantly,

"Bingo John. The print matches."

I almost jump out of my own skin. My heart is beating so fast that I feel light-headed. Mona can tell I am excited, and I open my mouth to respond.

She holds her finger up to stop me and she continues,

"I am sorry to say, but I have a positive match on Tommy's prints in our database." She stares at me hard to make sure she has my attention, "the print that matches the one from page three, is NOT Tommy."

She stands, balls her right hand into a fist and punches me in the arm,

"It was a great bit of detective work though. Whomever touched that woman, also touched this bottle, John."

She stares at me with an excited look on her face.

"Now what"? She says.

I am so excited and frankly troubled that I start to zone out. What IS next?

I tell her to PLEASE keep it quiet while I consider how to unveil this to the others. I then decide it's time to grab Arvind and Andrea. We need to think-tank this a bit.

Who touched that bottle and what do I do with the information?

I sit with Mona for a few minutes and gobble down my salad. Seems like a total waste of time to do this but Roku INSISTS it is the right thing to do.

I finish as quickly as I can and lightly punch mona in the arm, like she did to me earlier.

"OK, ten salads and we are going to another winery soon. Got it!" I blurt with a "see you later" tone.

Mona, with a mouth full of salad grunts to me, holds her finger up as if to say, "hold-on" and swallows. Then she continues,

"AND a really great *massage*." She smiles and goes right back to her seemingly bottomless salad.

I nod, laugh, and exit the lab. I hear her shout to me as I am in the hall,

"NOT joking!"

I need to clear my head, so I grab a coffee and stare out the window for a while. I then decide to walk through my own process for next steps. I want to try and work out some things on my own before I bring it to the other fish. I even close the fish video with Roku in mid-sentence. I am sure he is pissed at me for that.

With some thoughts of my own in place, I head back to my desk and start the discussion with Arvind, Andrea and Roku, the NON-digital versions.

Arvind is the first to engage me,

"John, you know, we are basically all the same brain so, no need to be so introspective here. It is just wasting time".

Andrea swims to-and-fro laughing at the comment.

Arvind continues,

"It's not Tommy. Unless our theory about the cause of death is wrong, which I am pretty sure we are not. So, we need to go back to the file and take a fresh look."

Andrea pipes in,

"Better yet, I suggest we talk about the bottle chain of custody. Who touched it from the very beginning until John handed it to Mona?"

I nod at Andrea as I agree with that thought process.

I am distracted by movement in the tank. The crab moves at the bottom of the aquarium, and I steady myself for a new voice to enter our foursome. I have been expecting this. I am sure I heard right when one of the fish stated, "the four of us are here to help you" or something close to that.

I continue to stare at the crab, waiting. The little creature skitters across the bottom and comes to a stop in front of where I am bent down staring. It just stares at me and does not say a damn thing. I think to myself, "*OK crab, whenever you are ready.*"

Andrea interrupts my focus on the crab with a subtle,

"Ahem," and continues, "Let's start at the beginning. Where is it bottled? We look there for anyone that may be of interest. We follow up with the distribution or delivery of the bottle to the tasting room. How did it get there? Once we have that, we can have a list of people that *could* have touched it."

I am scribbling notes on my pad looking up to see if anyone in the station is paying attention to my fish-tank fixation.

Andrea is swimming back and forth in a frantic pace. I wonder, is that in my mind and to someone else the blue fish is just gliding along as usual?

Andrea certainly loves this. It is right in her personality profile sweet spot.

She continues,

"Once we establish the human-chain of the bottle to the point that it reaches the tasting room, we will have a comprehensive list that we add the tasting room employees to. That is our starting point." She concludes.

Arvind swims forward with his body slightly puffed-up more than usual, and adds,

"Our outlier condition is anyone at the tasting room or chain of custody that could have touched the bottle that is not an employee or person of usual contact. That would include non-essential employees to the bottle, cleaning crews, etc. It will also include the customers at the tasting room."

Seems to me this is a straight-forward action. Makes sense and I am feeling pretty good about the thing I need to complete. I look over at Raines who is digging through a bunch of files while standing next to Skarsgard. I can't help wondering where they are on this thing. I am sure I will hear at the morning brief tomorrow, but I am going to need to bring them in and soon. It is starting to feel right.

My only problem is, the longer I wait, the harder it is.

I have lingered near the aquarium a bit too long. I tell the fish I am going to get started and will bring up "video chat" later.

This makes Roku laugh.

As I begin to exit the station, I notice Skarsgard looking at me oddly. I ignore it, but it stresses me out a little. I bet she is wondering what I am wasting my time on. Maybe I should just tell her and Raines about my theory NOW.

I prefer not to.

I am starting to want this. It is border-line intoxicating. My own investigative theory is forming. Like a REAL detective for once.

I hear a voice screaming at me from the tank. Its Andrea.

"John, remember, find Tommy first. Ask him if he ever met either of these gals."

I begin to drift back towards the tank and decide it better left to the cell phone recording "video-chat".

I open my phone and stand in the station parking lot as the fish come into view as I clarify.

"Ok, but why would I do that versus the bottle chain of custody?" I ask Andrea.

She replies,

"Because I think we want to try and paint the tasting room as ground-zero, NOT the bottle manufacture or distribution. It's my hunch, but if we can place the gals there at ANY point, we can potentially have something more than circumstantial conditions when we tell Raines". She continues, "Regarding Tommy, one would think he would have told the detectives on the case about it so it would be in the report, but, since it is not, we must question him directly. If he saw them at the tasting room, WHY didn't he say so?" She says.

Good point, I think to myself.

Arvind's voice chimes-in once she is finished,

"It is possible they were there at times Tommy did not work, so let's not get too wrapped up in that narrative, yet. Especially if he did NOT see them."

We all seem to agree on that point. I hold the phone down and squeeze my temples with my other hand.

I consider how pissed Skarsgard is going to get if she finds out I am chasing this without her. Especially since it has now just gotten VERY real.

I say as much to the fish, they just ignore me. Roku is the only one to chime in.

"John, deal with your own *internal politics* however you need to. But know that we are on the right track in my opinion, with these next steps. Skarsgard is another issue entirely. Deal with that later."

I stare at the phone a little confused. That was an odd comment. My own "internal politics." What-the-fuck does that mean? So, because I like Skarsgard, does he think I am using Mona and leading her on?

I decide that trying to unwrap what Roku meant is decidedly too complicated for me to manage right now. Romance always makes things so complicated, EVEN when the people, er, FISH calling me out on it are doing so in my own imagination. It just annoys me.

Man, I am such a weird dude.

I put my phone back in my pocket and head for the coastal access areas. That is where Tommy is.

SIX

I head for the area where the ranger's usually patrol. The local access spots, where the commerce is, will be where the local PD patrols. The Park Rangers will spend most the time at the coastal areas that are given national park status or near protected wildlife zones. I start there at a massive, but beautiful, oceanside rocky tidepool area called Cuevas de la Luna, or translated, *Caves of the Moon*.

The coastal national park is named for the alien looking formations and breathtakingly beautiful scenery that seems to glow in the moonlight.

While perusing the groups of people, I feel lucky to see a uniformed park ranger. I take a few moments to gather my thoughts on how to engage this series of questions as I slowly walk toward the ranger.

When I get closer, I realize it is not Tommy, but instead another ranger, an older man named Art Sullivan. Tall, lean, and pale, Art seems even more pale due to his jet-black dyed hair. He gives off an almost vampire-like vibe due to his stature and general creepy disposition.

I make my visit with the odd man short and inquire towards where I can find Tommy. He tells me that Tommy is positioned in the same area for the next few days due to a hatching of a special bird. The endangered species called the Snowy Plover has taken up residence off a coastal access point to the beach. The rangers rope it off, but in general, it requires a uniformed sentry to make sure no one bothers the birds due to how sensitive they are at the newborn stage. Tommy can be found there.

When I arrive, the small parking lot is full of people entering the local beach spot. Tommy is standing right at the mouth of the access point and is telling stories to people about local lore. Things like wine, soil, animals, anything that folks find interesting. It sounds like Tommy knows a lot about the area.

So, not only handsome, but knowledgeable.

He ends every story with his warning to stay to the left of the beach, away from the roped off portion. He explains about the rare birds and warns of a $500 fine that he himself can enforce.

I wait for roughly twenty minutes as he finishes talking to a family of European visitors. The father seems a little irritated at the wife as they enter the beach. Must have been how much attention she drew from Tommy, or perhaps gave to him.

Tommy makes eye contact with me and walks to greet me.

"Hello detective Fitch."

I am now annoyed even further by his knowing my right name. He is just too much. Next thing you know he is going to invite me over for BBQ and Cigars. He reminds me of that pro football quarterback that has that perfect wife and keeps winning Super-Bowls. The guy that played until he was like 50-years old.

Roku chimes in as I am leering at Tommy and about to engage him in conversation,

"Everyone loves to hate the winners and the pretty people John. Might want to give this guy a break."

I am irritated by Roku's voice, and I look down to find my phone in my hand with the fish video looping. Wow, I did not even know I started it.

Frustrated that I can't reply, I just shake Tommy's hand and begin to question him. He is oddly transparent and seems to have zero concern about the questioning. Cool. Maybe too cool.

I hear Roku again,

"John, stop it!"

FUCK, OK fine. This guy is great. *I'll just buy a "Team Tommy" shirt and hang out with him at bars while he picks up chicks*, I think to myself.

I spend roughly ten minutes with Tommy and come to the end of it. Turns out, the second young woman, the one found with the partial print on her neck (my best clue) in the meadow, Tommy met at the winery. He says, not only that, but he saw her several other times near Cuevas de la Luna when he and "Lurch" were working the area together. He calls ranger Sullivan the sarcastic nick-name due to his ghoulish look and long rangy appearance. It also turns out that he mentioned this very same fact to Raines, but it did not make it into the report. Tommy does not seem to know why but seems unconcerned about it.

I prepare to leave, and head to the tasting room and Tommy seems to get awkward for a moment. He starts to talk and then pauses, seeming to compose himself.

Roku is all over it,

"Hang on John. He is about to tell you something and it is of concern to him. May be something relevant since he is hesitant."

I gesture openly for him to continue, trying to look unconcerned and comforting.

He then pulls out his small pad from his shirt pocket as he asks the question.

"If you and Mona aren't exclusive, would you mind if I asked you for her contact info? I want to give her a call."

Roku groans and I just stare at Tommy with a bewildered look. I try and answer him politely, but I am so pissed I just blurt,

"She is a cop. Just dial 9-1-1".

Tommy looks at me genuinely taken back by my attitude.

So, Tommy is handsome, knowledgeable, genuinely nice, and SHOCKINGLY low on emotional intelligence.

Ladies and gentlemen, Tommy, the Deity of love and protector of endangered fucking BABY BIRDS!

Only one-word forms in my mind as I leave, and I decide to cleansingly shout it out loud when I am out of earshot.

"MOTHERFUCKER!"

My next stop is the tasting room. On my way, I pull out my phone, start charging it and open the fish video.

Arvind is the first to engage me. He is lost in thought while speaking.

"It is not totally sketchy, but why did Raines not put all of that into his notes?"

Andrea has a pretty good retort, but it leaves us a bit concerned still.

"Because he expected YOU John to be the detailed report guy. Did he give you any notes to add to yours?"

I don't recall any and I tell the fish this fact. I will have to get into this with him when I bring both he and Skarsgard into the mix, which I am just about ready to do.

Tasting room first and then I will write it all up and get the big three involved, including captain Bradley.

As I exit the Moonscape area, my natural path takes me through a small beach front area with a long pier that allows people to fish and is usually a place to get some exercise. The area is always crowded this time of year, during the spring wave and today is no exception. My favorite restaurant is located here, and I realize that I am getting a little hungry. The *Earth Room*, named for the natural and sustainable way they grow their own herbs and vegetables, has great morning food, but also good lunch sandwiches. The chicken and pork are locally raised and hormone free, making this a pretty good place to meet the more *natural* type. Guys wearing flip-flop sandals and jeans with gals that are not overly fixated on make-up. Not exactly the hippy type but a more nature loving, and Earth concerned crowd. I tend to feel relaxed and welcomed around the folks here. Not sure if that makes me a naturalist but, I do not EVER show anyone my toes. It's a real hang-up of mine.

As I walk up to order a sandwich, I notice the jolly bear of a man that Mona and I met at the tasting room is set-up near the coffee house next door to my lunch spot.

I walk up to the cupcake king; Drew Booth and he does not seem to recognize me.

I greet him and start to hatch a plan to delight Mona with a box of cupcakes.

He is genuine and excited to sell his cakes as he was at the tasting room. He offers me a cross section of assorted flavors that pair very well with the coffee offered inside the shop.

I know that Tommy won't know about Mona loving these cupcakes. Drew is my new secret weapon.

I accept the cup of purified water he gives me to "clear my palate" and I head over to get my lunch with a box of six cupcakes in tow.

This was a great sidebar.

A short twenty minutes later I take a long gulp of the water and I exit my vehicle. I enter the tasting room which is vacant of anyone except for the wine maker and another management employee of the winery. Turns out both men are brothers.

I flash the badge and we three sit and have a pointed discussion about wine, bottling and the supply chain.

I keep my phone open and my fish video feed on. Knowing Arvind, Andrea and Roku are listening.

The facts are simple. The wine bottles are received at the winery and promptly washed and sterilized. This is key. The fact, by itself, eliminates anything in the chain of custody BEFORE the winery itself. The winery has seventeen various people that work there and may come in contact with wine bottles. This includes drivers and case packing folks. The tasting room has a subset of the exact same people working, meaning, no one at the tasting room does not work at the winery, except one person. The red headed host.

I look at her and she seems to realize that we are all talking about her. Her name is Stephanie, and she is a local college student, working mostly evenings and weekends, except for today.

I ask for a comprehensive list of all the employees and offer a brief explanation as to why I am asking. I am not totally honest, but I indicate that it is law enforcement business, and I would be glad to get a warrant if they are resistant. I expect they will be.

Turns out, it is my lucky day, and they are happy to give me the employee roster, all the way to the top. Eighteen employees between the winery and the tasting room here in the Alleyway.

I can use this data to check for records, pull prints (if on file) and even get a warrant to take prints from them if my reason is strong enough. I think I have a good and substantial case for a top person of interest from this group. Once we get to who it is, we can take a long, close look at them. This is by no means the whole case, but it gives us a good suspect to start with.

I like where I am at on this one. I am now officially ready to talk to the other detectives.

Seven

Skarsgard stares blanky at me as I begin to speak. Raines is standing near the white board in our little bullpen regarding me with a cold look.

Skarsgard is the first to speak,

"I wondered where you have been going and what you have been doing. Slippery Devil you are."

Raines, irritated, nearly interrupts her as he says,

"You know, would not have hurt to tell me where you are going these past few days and maybe keep up on the other things we are working on."

I hold my hands up to both of them as if to say *Mia Culpa.*

"I know, I know, but I had to pull the thread and see where it went. I do not want to make drama and I realize the new guy gets scrutinized a bit more than you guys do."

Raines, shakes his head side to side in an argumentative way,

"So, I understand this clearly, you ran with what you are going to show me alone because I am overly critical of you? All of us here? captain Bradley?"

He looks at his shoes as he continues,

"Come on man."

Skarsgard tries to break the ice, looks back at Raines and pokes a jab at both of us,

"I don't know, I think he is a pretty big idiot myself Raines." She finishes with a laugh and prompts me to get on with it.

I just love hearing her slight Norwegian accent. It usually only comes out when she is speaking less formally.

Raines continues to stare at me, waiting for me to continue.

I clear my throat, grab another cup of water, and gather myself, just in time for captain Bradley to join. She gets the abbreviated layout from Raines and now all three of them are staring at me.

I lay out the entire series of hunches, ideas, and actions I took to reach this point. At the fingerprint, Raines shifts irritably, while captain Bradley and Skarsgard just stare at me.

The big reveal is the partial print, the wine bottle caper revealing a match and the bottle chain of custody.

Raines is first to speak, albeit grudgingly he sounds like he likes my pitch.

"Birdy, I like it. Its decent work. The chain of custody of that bottle and the target list is all very competent.," he looks at captain Bradley as he pauses, "The problem I have is that the print is a low priority lead. In fact, I saw the print and ignored it for the time being as it is not only highly circumstantial, but also highly likely to be a print matched with a first responder checking pulse."

He shifts uncomfortable while looking back at me directly.

"The other problem is that the print is only found on one victim. Meaning, unless something else connects the prints owner to the second victim, it does not link."

He walks over to me and claps a hand on my shoulder.

"You make some good points and chased it down while I sat on it. It is good work. Let's run the prints on first responders and known people at the scenes, like those field workers. We can at least confirm that and start on another thread while doing it."

I watch captain Bradley and Raines leave while waiting for Skarsgard to say something. Anything.

She just stares at me.

I lower my head and slap the table with my palm out of frustration.

"How could I have not checked the first responders. I did not even consider that based on the location of the print it was a likely pulse check".

Skarsgard continues to look at me thoughtfully and finally stands and walks toward me.

"It was a little bit of a miss; it may still come out a pretty darn good clue and one that we have a grip on. I think I like where we are John. I like it a lot."

I look up at her and feel a moment of hope and get a little lost in her eyes, as usual. I appreciate her downplay of my logic miss.

The funny part is, Andrea and Arvind also missed it. In fact, my code breaking genius is the one that fixated me on it.

I growl to myself as I head over to the tank.

After a brief but spirited review with the three fish, Andrea seems unconcerned.

"John don't miss the key point to our assumptions at the time when we discovered the print. I said it was a thumb. Pulse checks are done on that portion of the neck with the more sensitive pointer and middle fingers."

She drifts over to float directly in front of me as she continues.

"Of course, I considered that. But the other key item is that the print is from the hillside victim and that body was found quite a while after death. Meaning, the first responders or field workers would not have likely felt the need to do a vitals check. Wrong fingers, wrong timing."

Ah Andrea. Just like that I am back in the hopeful place I was prior to the update session.

How could I have EVER doubted Andrea.

It is later in the evening and Raines waves me over. Skarsgard and captain Bradley are already walking to where he is.

The first responder prints were NOT a match. Like Andrea suggested they would not be.

Raines has a bit of gumption as he tells us this fact. I think he is excited. Skarsgard opens her mouth to speak, and captain Bradley interrupts her.

"This is outstanding. Especially given the wine bottle find."

I jump in with Andrea's narrative around the thumb print and state of the body at the time of finding.

I also add in my own two cents on the thumb being a prominently more powerful digit. Meaning, one you would use to hold something closed, LIKE an ARTERY!

captain Bradley insists we go home and rest. Now that we are all on the same page, she is planning on opening this up the next day and wants us all well rested. No mistakes due to being tired.

As I leave the station, something is tickling the back of my mind. I am troubled at how the captain interrupted Skarsgard. In fact, Skarsgard seems to be taking a back seat on this, versus how aggressive she usually engages things. I almost feel like she is doing it on purpose. My instincts are suggesting to me she knew I was chasing something down and wanted me to get some spotlight. Not sure why this even enters my head, but it is something to consider.

I spend the night staring at the ceiling. Going over and over things. We need to get the eighteen people's prints. That is where we find our top suspect. When that is complete, we can dig into the person, run background, look for priors, determine vicinity to murder scenes based on cell tower bounces, etc.

So many great options on this one.

All we need is a print match.

The next day captain Bradley reveals that she has warrants issued for all eighteen employees prints IF she needs them. She is immediately getting prints for those that are not already in the system on a form of accessible record. DMV, or another other form of public profile that requires it.

Good news is fifteen of the people were either on DMV record, prior arrest record or involved in local youth sports which require background check and fingerprinting. The bad news for our case, is that all fifteen are clear.

The other three people will be processed within a few hours and get checked. Raines, and I are climbing the walls waiting on this, while Skarsgard is nowhere to be found. Probably picking up the slack on other cases.

I look around for my notebook and padfolio and realize I must have left it in my car. I NEVER go anywhere without it. Man, I must be dazed.

I will have to get it before the morning meeting. I am VERY meticulous about how I take notes. They must be on my pad with my specific pen.

I walk over to the aquarium and spend a few minutes staring at the little crab. The fish watch me silently and the crab does absolutely nothing. I want so badly to get this out of the way. Each of these disassociated entities is vastly different. What if the crab is a jerk, or causes me more anxiety than having this disorder already does?

Just then the crab begins to move and walks over to me. Its stalked eyes look straight at me. Staring at me like I am staring at it. It raises its pincered arm and touches the glass.

Suddenly captain Bradley enters the room, and my focus is immediately back on the case.

She beckons Raines and I to come join her at the white board.

She talks directly to ME, not Raines.

"All eighteen people are clear. We need to find someone else that could have touched that bottle." She growls before continuing, showing visible signs of frustration.

"Anyone that goes to that tasting room could have reached and grabbed that bottle. We may be heading toward a credit card and point-of-sale transaction review. This will capture some number people that have gone there."

Raines groans while nodding. He regards the captain with a calm look as he speaks.

"Better than nothing captain."

He then turns to me and points his finger at me.

"Make sure that bottle and the chain of evidence is clean. Make sure Mona processes it and everything is now above board. In fact, you need to state in the report that you are chasing down ranger Tommy as a person of interest. It is just cleaner that way, even though he is clear of this currently."

I nod and head to the car to grab my padfolio and then to the lab to talk to Mona, who is staring into a micro-scope.

When she notices me, she backs away from the scope, smiles and rubs her eyes.

"A little early for salad don't you think?" she says.

I give her a brief smile and then we spend the next few minutes going over the bottle and I relay the next steps to her.

I see that she still has several uneaten cupcakes left from the box I brought her, and she sees me staring at them.

"Want a several days old cupcake?" she says.

I laugh and offer to take her out for lunch. She accepts and we make a plan to get back together in a few hours.

Skarsgard is back at her desk looking at my expectantly.

"What did I miss?" She says.

I give her an abbreviated update after which she winks at me and gives me an "Atta-boy" thumbs up. Coming from her, it means a lot to me.

I go back to my notes and update the items Raines asked me to. I will add them to my report later.

EIGHT

Mona and I head to the Earth Room for a soup and sandwich combo and have a nice talk about non work stuff. I am wondering where exactly this thing between us is going, as I am sure she is also. Our friendly cupcake baron is out in front of the coffee house next door again and I can hear his laugh from the backyard ocean view patio, where we are seated enjoying our lunch.

The smell of the salty air and the sound of the ocean always helps me focus and I find it soothing in an otherwise high-pitched world I live in.

As we leave, of course Mona wants to grab more cupcakes. We head over and are happily greeted by Drew. He is excited to see Mona and offers her a special cupcake of the day, a teacake infused with lavender. We share it, AFTER (of course) clearing our palate with Drew's filtered cup of water. It is a small slice of heaven.

Mona, *of course*, buys a half dozen. She is also excited to learn that Drew Booth is going to be at one of the local night spots this coming Saturday night. It is a building that has a facade that has been designed to look like an old west saloon. It is a bit of a cowboy bar and lounge that doubles as the best source of club like nightlife in the Vista Tranquila area. Located conveniently right across the street from the Earth Room. Drew hands us a flyer that shows cupcakes, whisky, and micro brews. It says, "Saturday Night Karaoke sponsored by Drunken Cakes."

Mona eyeballs me expectantly and I sheepishly suggest that we should consider going, together. Her face erupts in a beaming smile, and we head back to my car.

As we reach my car, I spend a second or two looking at the ocean. I unlock the door and Mona gets into the car. She places her plastic water cup into the right-side cup holder. As I plop down into my seat, I realize I have nowhere to put mine. The cup from a few days ago is still in in the left-side cupholder in my car.

I see a trashcan about ten yards away and I reach for the empty cup to throw it away.

Suddenly my hand freezes. I stop cold. My mind explodes with a shocking realization. The cup, from the cupcake king. The same man that visits several local public hang outs, including the tasting room of the Onyx Mountain winery!

I drop my cup and water spills on the ground. I jump into the car and hurriedly make for the station. Mona seems startled by my sudden frenzy of activity.

"John are you OK?" she says. "What's wrong?"

I look at her with a smile and eyes glowing with excitement.

"Oh YEAH. I'm good. Whatever you do, DO NOT touch this cup!" I say, pointing to the water cup in my holder.

Mona looks at me, then at the cup, she seems baffled for a moment, then suddenly inhales with an audible gasp while covering her mouth with both hands.

I look at her, shaking my head up and down,

"Yeah, EXACTLY."

I grab my padfolio and start scribbling notes. My thoughts are pouring out onto the paper. I do not want to miss a single item that I am thinking on this.

We make it back to the station quickly and I run in to see if Raines or Skarsgard are available. Neither are there. I check my phone, no calls, texts, or even relevant emails. Where can they be?

I see the captain, who notices me and perks up. I am obviously jazzed, and she can see it. She hurriedly rushes out of her office to engage me. I notice I left my notes in the car. I hold up my finger and do a quick dance to get around Mona, who is standing by eagerly. I whisper to her,

"Not a word. I will be RIGHT back."

I rush out to my car, grab my padfolio, rush back inside and am delighted to find Skarsgard now seated at her desk. I get her attention with a loud "OY" to get her to join us.

I ask them where Raines is, and the captain says she can get him here quickly if needed, but urges me to fill her in.

I point to Mona, who is holding a pen inside of the upside-down cup that had been in my car. I point at it excitedly,

"Dollars to donuts our print is on this cup. And if it is, man, we have a primary suspect. It will blow your mind captain."

Both the captain and Skarsgard look at me steadily and neither speaks before Mona chimes in.

"I am going to go process this. We will know in a few minutes".

She runs off toward the direction of her lab.

I yell after her,

"For God's sake Mona, be careful!"

She waves a hand over her head and disappears around a corner.

Skarsgard asks me a bunch of questions, as if she had them all queued up. The captain also starts bombarding me. I hold up my hands as if to slow them down.

"Wait just a few minutes. Let's get the results first. Then, this thing is going to get interesting."

While we are waiting, I run over to the fish tank. I almost feel ashamed that I have not even opened my phone to discuss this with them. After all, they have been a key part of getting us here, wherever "here" actually is.

The fish swim up to me in a hurry. I go down the details of my thinking, piece by piece. I try and look like I am reading to myself so that anyone who has eyes on me don't think I am talking to the fish tank.

I get to the end of my theory, to this point, and Arvind seems to nod at me, if a fish can actually do that.

"See John, you did that completely on your own. And, I might add, it is not by any means a reach. It is wholly plausible."

Roku swims to the forefront and pushes past Arvind.

"You should now see that you ARE a good detective. You are making headway all on your own. I agree with Arvind."

Andrea excitedly pipes in as well,

"You do not always need us, John. And it is good that you didn't open your phone while being out with Mona. Even with these things falling into place This is real growth and it is a good next step."

I feel embarrassed. I am sure my face is red. My make-believe fish friends are complementing me, and I am embarrassed by it. What a loser.

I hear someone running down the hall and I look up to see both Skarsgard and captain Bradley look at me as they focus on the hallway commotion.

Mona quickly skids around the corner, a wild look on her face. She looks around the room for me and we lock eyes. The world seems to stand still, and my heart is nearly beating out of my chest.

I see Raines walk in the door of the station. He looks at all of us and obviously becomes aware that something is happening.

I look back to Mona. She stops in front of the four of us and shakes her head up and down. She squeaks out a barely audible word.

She swallows hard and tries again, but louder.

"It's a MATCH" she yells. "The prints match."

The man known to us as Drew Booth the "Cupcake King" and owner of "Drunken Cakes" is actually named Terrence James Daniels. The prints came back with a positive match and had pictures and detail to boot.

Terry Daniels thought he could hide-away in a sleepy little place like Vista Tranquila. Armed with a false identity, Terry escaped multiple charges of violent behavior and managed to remain at-large while having multiple warrants for his arrest.

Over the next days, the captain managed to easily get a warrant to search Drew Booth's place of residency and Drew was easy enough to get into custody while this action was underway. The warrants helped us hold him.

I walked into Mona's lab to find her still looking ill. Since the day Drew, or Terry, had become our primary suspect, Mona had been sickened that she ate his cupcakes and drank his water.

I look at her desk and find that she had not thrown away the cupcakes. She notices my perplexed look.

"Never know if these will be evidence of some kind, right?"

I smile at her and walk up behind her to give her the best neck and shoulder massage I could manage. Raines advice be damned.

A while later I walk back to the main station area near the captain's office and see Skarsgard sitting at her desk. She notices me and waves me over as Raines also sees me and yells to get my attention.

"Birdy. Time to go".

Captain Bradley, some suited man (likely the district attorney), Raines and I begin to leave the station. It is time for our formal search of Drew Booths apartment. We have been playing this very carefully.

As I exit the station, I look back at Skarsgard and see she is not coming. I ask the others to wait a moment as I go back to the bullpen to get her.

She sees me coming and stands to meet me.

"Hey, let's go!" I say.

She smiles at me. Hugs me and has tears in her eyes. She softly whispers in my ear,

"Not this time John. You have this all to yourself."

Perplexed, I push her away and look into her beautiful eyes. I look at her, then I notice the fish swim over to the side of the tank nearest to us.

Skarsgard reaches her hand up to touch my cheek.

"Don't worry. We will all be here when you get back."

She smiles and looks over her shoulder at the fish and back at me with a smile.

My brain catches fire and explodes. I cannot feel my arms. I stare in total shock at Skarsgard, now standing by the fish tank. I stare at her and at the damn crab.

"The...four...of us." I utter.

She smiles and nods.

I continue to stammer, trying to make sense of this.

"You aren't real?"

She points at my padfolio. I open it and reach inside. Paper, pen and of course, family photo.

I am confused.

I look closely at the photo and realize the friend of my mother and father, standing behind them to the left, looks nearly identical to Kari Skarsgard.

Skarsgard is one of my dissociative manifestations.

She touches my arm lightly and with a reassuring voice tries to calm me.

"We are as real as anything John. In your mind we are real. It does not matter if we exist elsewhere. I am more recent than the others, but everything we are, has been made by your mind. Your brilliant mind."

I look back and see the others waiting in the running vehicles out front.

She pushes me,

"GO. This is your time. You finish this by yourself. We are here if you need us."

I lay the photo on my desk, mind racing, so confused, so many questions. Skarsgard looks at the photo and smiles with an affirming nod.

As I back away, I say to her,

"You are different though. You are not an object or thing talking to me. You are a projection." I pause, considering what this means, "This means my condition is evolving."

I shrug. It is what it is. I remind myself, "I'm nuts!"

As I leave, I look at the crab in the tank and laugh. So, it WASN'T the crab.

"Well played crab. Well played."

All four of the others laugh as I head out the front door.

NINE

Drew Booth's apartment is nestled on top of a small industrial building. Inside the lower structure is a medium sized industrial kitchen space, which is used by multiple non-storefront food preparers. Mostly specialty delivery services or caterers. With Booth (or as we now call him Daniels-Booth) in custody, the small apartment located on the second floor is easy to process. The hope is that there will be enough here in the form of concrete evidence to place him at each crime scene. The apartment smells delicious. Booth has sugar-cookie flavored candles distributed throughout the apartment. This guy loved his baked goods. We spend an hour looking through the place and find nothing out of the ordinary.

Booth has a pantry full of industrial grade baking goods that he must not store in the downstairs shared space.

We look inside each container and find only the expected baking elements. I decide to open my phone and I start the video.

Arvind urges me to remove the big items from the pantry and do a wall and ceiling hidden cavity search. He and Roku think that it would not be unusual for Booth to have placed his enthusiastic items in a space together. Baking cupcakes (which are truly impressive) is his thing, so maybe, they suggest there is something elusive to be found in the pantry, where his trademark cupcakes are born.

The rest of the investigators begin to wrap up. Spending most the time gathering DNA type items like hairbrush, toothbrush, and the like, I am alone to peruse the pantry. As I knock on the walls and ceiling, checking for an empty space, I knock over a container of corn meal which falls to the floor. It lands with a hollow *thud* a foot in front of where I am standing. I pick it up and place it back on the counter and kneel to knock on the floor. The floor goes from solid to hollow as I knock. I shout for the others to join me, and we take a closer look at the flooring.

A small space measuring roughly a square foot has a well measured wooden cutout, Because the floor is hardwood, it is difficult to see because it is cut so precisely. There is also a screw holding down the small hatch-like piece. We get a screwdriver and carefully open the compartment, with video rolling. There is not much in the compartment. But, thankfully, based on what we find, not much is needed.

Three bottles, a small folder, and a few sandwich bags. The bottles are labeled, exactly as we had hoped, Flunitrazepam, Gamma Hydroxybutyric Acid (GHB) and Ketamine. All the ingredients for mixing the cocktail for doping people into a submissive, helpless state, while leaving them movement functional. The sandwich bags have small bunches of hair in them. Not enough that a coroner would have determined hair was cut or missing, just a few strands.

The real damning find for Terrence James Daniels is the photos. Old school instant Polaroid style pictures, one of each victim, taken just as they are dying or near death. Face clearly visible and Daniels-Booth's thumb pictured holding the artery closed.

The only problem is, there are five photos and five sets of hair.

We all realize there are still three victims we have not found and may never find.

The crime scene teams close off the apartment and gather the evidence. The captain, Raines and I leave to head back to the station. As we exit and reach the parking lot, there is a quiet moment. We all look at each other with a look of disgust. There is also another feeling, one that can only be described as a peaceful relief.

Raines looks at captain Bradley and says,

"Case closed!"

I open my video of the fish and it is Andrea that speaks to me, flanked by Arvind and Roku.

"The prosecution of this man will be easy. The biggest task is matching the three other ladies with recent missing persons from the nearby vicinity. I suggest going as far as Los Angeles to San Francisco."

Andrea is always here to solve puzzles. I am just not in the puzzle solving mood anymore. I nod in agreement, close my phone, and sit quietly and stare out the window of the SUV.

The three of us do not say a word as Raines drives back to the station.

I am invited to observe as Raines meets with Daniels-Booth in the interrogation room. The district attorney suggests we do not need a confession or any such thing. This case is airtight. Daniels-Booth has even waived the right to legal representation. Smartly, the D-A makes sure there is a public defender present. Daniels-Booth ignores everything the man tells him.

This seems like it will be nothing more than a ceremony. Yet, all three of us wants the closure of showing the evil man that he has been found, and we know who and what he is.

The bellowing laughter makes me sick to my stomach. The same laugh I would hear while he was peddling his cupcakes. Raines calmly and professionally covers all the bases. He informs Daniels-Booth that we have everything we need. Guilt is not up for debate. What we really want is the three other victim locations.

The large man continues to laugh without giving Raines anything useful.

I decide to open my phone and see what the fish think. Skarsgard, standing next to me smiles and says,

"Talk to Roku. This is his specialty."

I form a plan with Roku and tell the captain that I need five minutes and I will be right back. I urge her to give me a few minutes with Daniels-Booth.

I rush to my car, and I grab an old bag of snack mix that I have in a small sandwich bag. I head to my desk and grab a pair of small scissors and cut off a small portion of my hair. I clean out the bag and I place the hair in the bag.

I head back to the interview, in progress and I insert my Bluetooth earbuds into my ear so that Roku can speak through me. Lastly, I grab a long-necked lighter used for lighting candles and I knock on the door.

Raines lets me enter and stands back. I see him look at the one-way window, unsure what we are doing.

For the next two minutes, Skarsgard stands next to me and tells me exactly what to say and how to say it. She shows amazing interrogator skills that I do my best to encompass as I deliver her performance. Roku advises me of the impact, or lack thereof, that we are making on Daniels-Booth, who continues to laugh with indifference and seemingly genuine humor. He actually just thinks this is all very funny.

Finally, when the bear of a man does not crack, we go to plan B.

I pull out the bag of hair and show it to Daniels-Booth. He stops laughing. His face turns a bright shade of red and his eyes deaden. He grumbles to me,

"That is mine. That is not yours."

I open the bag and lay the hairs on the table in front of me.

Raines shift uncomfortably. Not being part of the plan, he is unaware that this is not the actual crime scene hair.

"Birdy, don't touch that!"

I follow Skarsgard's performance to stifle Raines aggressively. I strike the lighter and move toward the hair with it.

The big man's dark eyes lock onto me. A look of pure hate and evil, it is like staring at a shark. He struggles against his constraints.

I move a few strands to one side, and I burn them.

The man shrieks as if I am burning HIM.

Roku is all over it. He tells me what to do and how to do it.

I gather the rest of my hairs and I move toward it with the lighter.

I tell him this is the last time we will ask. Roku tells me to get everything out of him because NOW is the best chance we have. Skarsgard tells me how to posture myself and exactly what to say and do.

Raines, flipping out, only helps the false narrative.

Within five minutes, Daniels-Booth has confessed to each murder, given us details on how he did it and even told us where to find the two victims we can recover. The first victim is unrecoverable as she was dumped into the ocean when he had worked a booze-cruise down south.

Now we can finally say, case closed.

I stand up, exhausted. I push the hairs to Daniels-Booth.

"Here you go. You can keep these."

He bellows joyously, with his now infamous laughter.

I lean over and wordlessly show him a portion of my hair that is obviously missing and was hastily cut.

The man stops laughing and his shark like gaze stares daggers at me.

Wordlessly we conclude our business with each other. A bond formed between the hunter and the hunted as I hold his stare.

I cannot help it and decide to poke the bear. I lean in and whisper to him,

"The tea-cake and lavender cupcake, simply TO DIE for".

His dead eyes continue to stare at me, but I see the side of his mouth lift upward into a very slight smile.

OH, great. Here I thought I was being snarky, and I made him proud instead. Well, honestly though, they were *TO-DIE-FOR!*

Raines, Skarsgard and I exit the room and meet the district attorney and captain back in the main station bullpen area.

We conclude the day with a series of plans related to finding the missing ladies' bodies, which will not be done by our own department, and both the captain and Raines let me know that I get to document this all. After-all, I write the best reports.

Before she leaves, the captain extends me her hand, and she has a profound look of pride on her face as she speaks.

"Tomorrow, the papers will report all of this. You had better prepare yourself John. You are about to get a lot of attention."

Raines walks up beside me and claps his hand on my shoulder,

"Detective John Fitch, the man who caught the *Cupcake Killer!*"

I stare at him in surprise. He actually said my name correctly!

Raines, understanding my look and the weight of the moment, decides to break the ice.

"Come on Birdy," he pauses for effect, "That report is not going to write itself!"

TEN

Daniels-Booth cut a sweetheart deal. He will get a life sentence, avoid the death penalty and will be given access, under heavy guard, to bake once a month for three hours. Forever.

The key to the deal was his willingness to give the locations of the three other victims remains.

To some it was a small price to pay to forego a trial and find the other victims.

Truth is though, to me, life in prison seems like a light sentence for Daniels-Booth. The public defender was not a total buffoon after all.

The full confession had also factored into the laughing man's deal and sentencing, but still seems wrong somehow. AND he gets to bake on top of it all. I mean, who the fuck will eat a cupcake from the "Cupcake Killer?"

I stand near the fish-tank and pinch a little food into the tank for my besties. Skarsgard is sitting at the spot she always sits at, which is just a printer table. Funny how I never really noticed some of these details.

I open my phone and snap a short video of the fish-tank with the photo of my father and mother next to it. Getting them all in the SAME video.

Skarsgard watches me and says,

"Taking me with you digitally?"

I shrug and answer her,

"You never know. And I am not carrying my padfolio everywhere I go anymore."

She smiles and seems pleased by that.

Raines and I go over the open case files one by one and begin to update progress.

It is eerie how unimportant these things feel. I mean, after dealing with a double homicide, which was really five murders, how does one go back to the mundane crimes and misdemeanors that we face here in Vista Tranquila?

Raines begins to pack up his gear and bids me farewell for the day.

I stare at the fish-tank and find the swimming of the fish calming. Arvind bounces his puffer face against the glass, while both Andrea and Roku glide along beautifully in their bright blue and translucent white forms.

I try and remember that they are just fish. "*SURE they are.*" I laugh to myself.

I see Mona walk into the bullpen area. She stands next to me and lightly punches me in the arm.

"Does the hero detective have time to buy me dinner."

I smile and stand bolt upright. I reach out and touch her cheek lightly as I answer,

"That sounds absolutely perfect." I lock my eyes on hers for effect as I continue.

"As long as the HERO crime lab technician picks the place!"

She smiles and raises excitedly up on her tippy toes and claps her hands quickly. I LOVE how she does that.

I grab my gear and we begin to walk out.

Suddenly, I hear a rough grumbly voice call out from behind me. It is not a voice I am familiar with.

"Hey, don't forget her back rub. Know what I mean!"

I look behind me and do not see anyone. Skarsgard smiles and gestures toward the tank.

I stop and stare at the tank and see the little crab skitter up to the side of the glass, claws clacking enthusiastically. His stalked eye actually *winks* at me.

I look at Skarsgard and the fish and spread my arms out in a gesture of confusion. The fish all claim they are as surprised as I am. Skarsgard just shrugs.

I place my hands on my hips and nod while looking at the crustacean's beady stalked eyes.

"The crab actually talks?" I laugh out loud. "I mean, why not!"

I turn to leave, and I can't hold back my smile as I quietly say to myself,

"You have GOT to be kidding me!"

End

Glenn EJ Williams is an American author and business professional located in Southern California. When not active in his business ventures, he enjoys spending time with his wife and children, pursuing his passion for American muscle cars, collecting vintage comic books, and tasting whisky from around the world.

He can also be found riding dragons into the sunset, exploring distant galaxies, adventuring through fantasy landscapes or any other imaginative way he can develop better stories to provide his readers in the future.

Printed in the USA
CPSIA information can be obtained
at www.ICGtesting.com
LVHW041017011123
762372LV00063B/976/J

9 781669 851011